my itty-bitty bio

Ruth Bader Ginsburg

Published in the United States of America by Cherry Lake Publishing
Ann Arbor, Michigan
www.cherrylakepublishing.com

Reading Adviser: Marla Conn, MS, Ed, Literacy Specialist, Read-Ability, Inc.
Book Designer: Jennifer Wahl
Illustrator: Jeff Bane

Photo Credits: ©Naval History and Heritage Command/Catalog # NH 67731, 5; © Vyntage Visuals/Shutterstock.com, 7; ©Tradlands/Flickr, 9, 22; © Lynn Gilbert/Wikimedia, 11; © Javen/Shutterstock.com, 13; © European University Institute/Flickr, 15; © National Archives Catalog/ Local ID P04553-09, 17, 23; ©Montanasuffragettes/Wikimedia, 19; © Rob Crandall / Shutterstock.com, 21; Cover, 1, 8, 12, 14, Jeff Bane; Various frames throughout, ©Shutterstock Images

Library of Congress Cataloging-in-Publication Data

Names: Spiller, Sara, author. | Bane, Jeff, 1957-
Title: Ruth Bader Ginsburg / Sara Spiller, Jeff Bane.
Description: Ann Arbor, Michigan : Cherry Lake Publishing, 2019. | Series: My itty-bitty bio | Includes bibliographical references and index.
Identifiers: LCCN 2018034509| ISBN 9781534142695 (hardcover) | ISBN 9781534140455 (pdf) | ISBN 9781534139251 (pbk.) | ISBN 9781534141650 (hosted ebook)
Subjects: LCSH: Ginsburg, Ruth Bader--Juvenile literature. | Judges--United States--Biography--Juvenile literature. | United States. Supreme Court--Biography--Juvenile literature. | Women judges--United States--Biography--Juvenile literature. | Jewish judges--United States--Biography--Juvenile literature.
Classification: LCC KF8745.G56 S65 2019 | DDC 347.73/2634--dc23
LC record available at https://lccn.loc.gov/2018034509

Printed in the United States of America
Corporate Graphics

table of contents

About the author: Sara Spiller is a native of the state of Michigan. She enjoys reading comic books and hanging out with her cats.

About the illustrator: Jeff Bane and his two business partners own a studio along the American River in Folsom, California, home of the 1849 Gold Rush. When Jeff's not sketching or illustrating for clients, he's either swimming or kayaking in the river to relax.

my story

I was born in Brooklyn, New York. It was 1933.

164
U.S.S. ELLIS.

My parents worked hard. My mother **earned** money for her brother. She helped him pay for school. She told me school is important.

How do you help other people?

Later, I married a law student. We had a child.

I went to law school. It was hard work studying and raising a baby.

My peers were mostly men. They were mean to me.

They thought men were better students.

I didn't give up. I was the best in my class.

I became a **lawyer**. I taught at colleges.

I used my job to help everyone.

I wanted everyone to be treated the same.

Why are people treated differently?

There are nine **U.S. Supreme Court justices**. President Bill Clinton chose me to be one of them. We make important choices.

What choices do you make?

I want all workers to be treated well.

I fight for women and men. I believe women should earn as much as men. I believe men and women should have the same chances.

HANG IN THERE RUTH
WE NEED YOU!

I helped make **gay** marriage **legal**.

I’m over 80 years old, but I’m tough! I believe the laws apply to everyone.

What would you like to ask me?

1959

1930

Born
1933

1993

2030

glossary & index

glossary

earned (URND) to get money by doing work

gay (GAY) a person who is attracted to people of the same sex

lawyer (LOI-ur) a person who studied the law and is trained to help others in legal matters

legal (LEE-guhl) allowed by law

U.S. Supreme Court justices (YOO ES su-PREEM KORT JUHS-tis-iz) people who hear cases in the highest and most powerful court in America

index